October is the Time

Drew Christopher

DoDo Bros. Publishing
2019

October is the Time

First Printing: 2019

ISBN 978-1-67813-948-3

Dodo Bros. Entertainment
1703 N 3rd St.
Grand Forks, ND 58203

www.<Your Internet Address>.com

Contents

Acknowledgements

I would like to thank my teachers, my English classmates, and my family without whose help this book would never have been completed.

Thank you for your patience and guidance, your use of the red pen…

Chapter 1: The Ribbon

October is the time to protect yourself from what is out there. This dreaded month of Halloween, the month of…....

Josh lost his train of thought and started over on his English paper. He was a creative person but when it came to putting his ideas on paper he usually got stuck.

The month of terror and depression; it is the time when the worst comes out in people, it is..... A thud on his window startled him, he sat back quietly for a minute to see what would happen. All that could be heard was the wind and the chilling call an owl in the distance. The window shook with another thud and he got up from his chair to investigate. He watched as a black bird flew right into the glass window with another thud. Curious, he went outside to see what happened to the bird. He peered everywhere but found nothing and went back inside to continue his essay. The next morning while getting ready for school, Josh asked his family if they heard or seen anything from the prior night. But, to his surprise, no one had heard anything except him going in and out of the house. He shrugged it off as he usually did when it came to his family's response to anything he says, and headed off to school. He opened the front door only to find a raven with a red ribbon around its neck, staring right at him from the roof of his dad's truck. He was a little spooked but didn't think much of it and kept walking.

The raven followed him slowly, from tree to tree. It would stare at Josh intensely. Being slightly annoyed, he stopped and looked at the raven. The large black bird creeped him out. Its beady black eyes felt like pools of inky oil, as if it could see into his soul, take his deepest fears and bring them to the surface. Coming back to reality, it'd became dead silent when the raven produced a horrifying squawk that shook the ground and echoed through the neighborhood.

Frightened from the raven's screech, Josh hurried away and this time the raven didn't follow him but its gaze did, tracking his every step. He looked back and the raven's eyes shone red… blood red. He went from speed walking to full on sprinting, before looking back one more time as the raven disappeared. He slowed down when he finally arrived at the school. Other than the occurrences of the morning, nothing else happened that day, but Josh couldn't stop thinking about the raven. Its eyes and how they made him want to just crawl into a ball and die, right there on the sidewalk. How he believed the ribbon around its neck must mean something and how about why it followed him down five blocks. Josh might have been a strange kid. But, he had never felt this way before.

He ran the whole length back to his house after school trying to avoid another encounter with the strange bird. Slowing down a little when he was about a block away from home, but he still couldn't stop the feeling of unrest, the feeling that something terrible would happen and wouldn't be able to do anything about it, like he was going to die right there and then.

His thoughts were interrupted by the sight of a rabbit on his lawn, it was apparent that it had the same red ribbon around its neck, or what was left of it. As he got closer it was apparent that the poor creature had no head, its body soaked in blood, Josh could only tell that it even had a ribbon by the blood being significantly darker that the hue of the cloth.

The same horrific squawk from that morning rang in the distance, Josh dashed inside and into his room. Having never heard such a terrifying sound before that day. The thought of the bird made him go to the attic and grab his gun. He had no idea why, but he felt like he might need it.

When his parents came home, they opened his door to see Josh on his bed wielding a fully loaded double barrel shotgun pointed right at them. “SON, DON’T SHOOT!” his dad bellowed as he got closer to take the firearm away from his son. He grabbed the gun and unloaded the buck shot onto the floor. “What in the hell is wrong with you boy, pointing a gun right at your door?” His dad’s words yanked Josh out of his horrified trance to say a simple comment, “I don’t know.”

At dinner, Josh’s family stared at him with great worry written on their faces, carefully eating their food and watching him to make sure he wasn’t going to do something crazy.

“Soooo, how was everyone’s day?” Mrs. Oliver asked in acknowledgement of what had happened that afternoon. No one spoke but Mrs. Oliver started to talk about her day. As she relayed the events of her job Josh fell into another horrified trance... in a single blink of the eye his deepest fears flashed before him. He broke the trance to find that everyone was done and cleaning up from dinner. With a full plate of food, he went to the kitchen and put what was left in a Tupperware dish and stuck it in the fridge.

He went up the stairs only to hear his parents talking about that evening, “We need to hide all of the firearms from that boy. He is unstable. I don’t want to wake up in the morning with a glock to head”, Mrs. Oliver whispered back, “No, what we need to do is take him to a therapist. Something could be wrong! What if he has a mental illness?” Mr. Oliver retaliates. “That’s none of our business! What is our business is making sure he doesn't kill us in our sleep.” Mr. Oliver says this before noticing that Josh was on the stairway. Skeptical, he closed the master bedroom door. Josh continued walking up the stairs to his room where he softly closed the door. He tried to sleep, but the feeling that something terrible would happen kept him up all night. Every time he closed his eyes the raven and its ribbon haunted him. His heart pounding at the thought of its squawk, Josh didn't sleep at all that night.

In the morning, he went down to the kitchen to see his father locking all the firearms from the attic into the basement vault. Mr. Oliver looked Josh right in the eyes as he turned the last lock and kept staring at Josh as he walked out of the kitchen. Josh grabbed a pop tart from the pantry and left cautiously through the front door. The raven wasn't there, but he could still feel its presence.

Wearily, he walked to school finding neither a raven nor a rabbit, but Tim, his mailman, on someone's lawn just two blocks away from his own. He ran up the lawn to see if the man was ok, turning the mailman over with horror on his face. The man's face had no skin on it, just bloody muscle tissue and ligaments, cartilage from his nose in shreds, his ears barely hanging from his head. His eyes were cloudy white, limbs limp and body warm. Josh screamed in terror as the lifeless corpse's mouth fell open to show a red ribbon tied to its tongue. Josh yelled for someone, not a single person was around. He looked at the house and saw the curtains in the window move. He quickly ran to the gas station two blocks down and told the girl at the till to call 911, he then went to school with even more terror than he had had the day before. *October is the time of Terror.... To be scared, everything is dangerous, even your own mind.*

Chapter 2: The Blood

After school he walked back home to see the whole police squad blocking the neighborhood. He squinted to see the girl from the gas station at that house pointing towards him. Then a police officer came over and told him he was under arrest. His parents drove by to witness their son in handcuffs, being put into a squad car. Mrs. Oliver was in tears while Mr. Oliver had no expression at all.

At the Police station, he was brought to an interrogation room and left there alone. The room went dark, an inky blackness emanated from the walls, the screams of others ringing in his ears. The door then opened and an officer entered as the room went back to normal, it became completely silent except for the officer moving a chair to sit down.

The officer set down a manila folder with the name *Timothy Jacobs* typed on it. He looked up at Josh and spoke, "Do you know why you are here, son?" Josh tilted his head and said nothing. "You called the police for a supposed murder on your neighbor's lawn but, when we got there, there was nothing. No one in the house, no blood on the grass, just graffiti on the bathroom mirror saying *Josh Oliver did this* and a blood soaked ribbon on the sink. Can you explain that?" Josh looked up at the officer confused. "I swear, the mailman was dead on the lawn, and I didn't even come close to the house." The officer's eyes turned blood red and the darkness appeared again. The officer revealed hundreds of small sharp teeth, his smile at Josh was disturbing, voice demonic, "I know, I just wanted to see what you remembered". The officer lunged at Josh as he screamed in a high pitched wail. Josh screamed and the room snapped back to normal, the officer sat regularly in the chair. "Are you okay? All I did was ask your name." The officer said, in a frightened tone. Josh looked around and saw that nothing had apparently happened.

While cautiously looking at Josh, the officer raised his radio to his mouth and called for someone to take Josh out of the room. Two more officers came in the room and asked Josh to go with them, as he left the room Josh looked back at the first officer as his head turned one hundred and eighty degrees with red eyes and rows of sharp teeth.

The officer licked his teeth with his long blue tongue and snapped his head back normally. Josh tried to address this to the other officers but they wouldn't listen and kept on walking.

They brought him to a padded room that had nothing but mattress material on the walls and floor and a singular white arm chair. The officers coaxed him in and closed the door, which had a tiny viewing port two inches above Josh's chest. He sat down in the chair and sighed, thinking how shitty his week has been, he will never forget the trauma he has gone through.

A dripping sound can be heard from the corner of the room, he lifted up his head to have something drip on his face. Josh wiped it off only to see that it was blood, warm blood. Blood started dripping down all the walls. As he looked around, the padding on the walls started to burst with steaming organs, everything soaked in blood and guts. The whole incident left him so shocked he was paralyzed with a wide eye stare and an open mouth. He broke the paralyzation to have a piece of liver land right in his mouth, the taste caused him to vomit all over the room, the sight was wretched, not a single part of this now demolished room wasn't covered in a dark red color, guts or vomit.

With a dizzy head, Josh took one more look at the Grotesque scene before blacking out.

Josh woke up in a hospital bed with wires and IVs connected all over him. His hands were covered in blood and he felt super weak. He looked around the room and saw that on the nightstand next to the bed was a dead rose with a red ribbon tied around it. He turned his head to the left to see that raven with its oily black eyes and the same type of ribbon on its neck. Josh freaked out as a doctor carrying a syringe entered the room, Josh tried to get up but the doctor shoved him down. The doctor had the same red eyes and rows of tiny sharp teeth as the officer did, with a psychopathic look on his face he tried to force the syringe into Josh, he kicked the doctor in the face with all his strength, knocking him back. As Josh found his way out of the bed the doctor regained its balance, grabbed Josh and tried to stab him again, Josh struggled and stabbed the doctor with his own syringe right in his throat. The doctor let go of Josh and started to shake violently, his eyes turned white, foam dripping from the mouth. Josh ran out of the room as this scene unfolded.

He ran out of the hospital room door to find that the rest of the hospital was basically destroyed, vines growing on the walls, not a single unbroken light bulb, and no living creature in sight. Josh turned toward the room to see the lifeless corpse get up and stare right back at him, flesh melting from its body, blood oozing from the injection site. Josh slowly stepped back as the rotting corpse ripped open its chest cavity and broke off one of its ribs. Josh sprinted as the undead creature chased him with the sharp edge of its broken rib. Josh grabbed a bedpan and slammed it into the zombie's face, knocking it over as Josh continued to run.

As he ran, everything around him turned into nothingness, the void ever growing. He could hear the sound of the raven mocking him, the squawk echoing in his head, the raven stopped only to be replaced by ringing in his ears and the worst headache he has ever had. It drove him crazy, he started to pull out his hair, his scalp bloody from his own doing. "WHY! WHY ME?!" he shouted as he fell to the ground, he closed his eyes as he got covered in some wetness. Josh opened his eyes to see that he was in a puddle of blood, in some sort of dungeon like surrounding. Torches lined the walls of cobblestone and brick, the smell of rotting flesh and death was sickening, and he could see rats scurrying in the spilled blood, fighting over the bodies that surround Josh.

Josh stood up and looked around to see the bodies on the floor were those of his family, his brother's chest infested with maggots, his sister's eyes being eaten by rats, and his poor mother's skull bashed open with a steel pipe that laid right next to it. He was revolted by the sight and he vomited right on the corpses, which scared the rats away. He fell to the ground and sobbed uncontrollably, between sobs he noticed that his father wasn't there, there was no trace of him. Josh could hear walking behind him, he turned around to see a demonic looking thing with his father's face. He hurried against the wall as the thing walked closer. With a voice that could kill, the demon spoke to Josh, "Quite the sight, boy? They never saw it coming. I was waiting for you to come, so I could finish the job." The demon picked up Josh by the arms and started to pull them apart, his shoulders popped out of place, he could feel his skin and muscle tearing. Josh screamed in agony, he couldn't feel his fingers anymore and his arms were covered in his own blood.

With whatever strength he had left, Josh back kicked the demon-father hybrid in the chest, dropping him in the process. The air got knocked out of him, with internal bleeding setting in and no feeling at all in his left arm, he felt helpless. Josh weakly looked around and the demon was nowhere to be seen, with probably his last chance of survival, he got up and hobbled over to a door in front of him. Josh body slammed the door which opened to reveal the kitchen from his own house. Relieved, he ran in and slammed the door shut.

Josh quietly hobbled up the steps to his parents' bedroom to see his father in bed with another woman. He creeped up to his father's nightstand and saw that his father's hand gun was out, he grabbed the Smith and Wesson twenty-two pistol and loaded it. Mr. Oliver woke up to see his bloody headed, mangled armed son in a hospital gown pointing a gun right at his head, he moved to grab his son's arm and with a sharp bang Josh had shot his father right in the chest. The room went black; Josh in confusion and with a ringing in his ears, closed his eyes and opened them to see that he was at his desk with a sharp pain in his chest. He put his hand to his chest to find that he in turn was the one whom had been shot, he slowly turned around to find his father with a smoking barrel pointed at him and a red ribbon on his neck. Josh muttered a single phrase before his painful demise, “You Bastard”.

October is the time to be wary of your surroundings…. To trust nobody, everyone is the enemy, even your own mind.

Chapter 3: The Gun

Stephen looked right at the gun with a confidence that scared him, the gun that he just used to murder his son, his eldest child and he just looked at it. He spent a whole minute just looking at it, then lowered it and set it on the dresser. With no sign of a reaction, he grabbed his son's lifeless corps and hoisted it onto him shoulder, walked out of the room, turned off the lights and closed the door. He lugged the body all the way to the car in the garage and put it in the trunk with a cinder block, a jug of gas and some rope. He got in the car and drove down the driveway and three blocks down to the first stop sign. At the stop, he put a Christmas CD in and cranked it up, despite it being the middle of October.

Stephen drove for an hour listening to the same Bing Crosby songs the whole way. He pulled up to a gate that said *Private Property: STAY OUT*, and shut off the car. He got out, took the body, cement brick, and rope from the trunk and threw them over the fence. He then proceeded to climb the fence and jump over to the other side. Stephen grabbed his son's body, throwing it over his shoulder and grabbed the other things. He walked for an hour through the forest he entered, constantly searching for anyone that might witness the events going down. Stephen finally arrived at a small lake and dropped the corps onto the ground right at the shore. He walked away to come back dragging a small rowboat into the water, he loaded the body into the boat and headed toward the middle of the lake.

Once he got near the middle, he tied one end of the rope to his son's ankle and the other end to the cinder block. He threw the body into the water and then dropped the cement, dragging his son to the bottom. Stephen stared into the distance when he saw a raven fly and land on the bench of the boat. The eerie bird had a ribbon around its neck and its eyes shone red, Stephen with no expression nodded and so did the bird, it flew away. He rowed back to shore, poured gas all over the vessel and threw in a match. Stephen walked away as fire consumed the boat. Screams could be heard from the forest as he walked through it, about ten minutes in has stopped on the trail and just psychotically yelled into the distance, and the screams stopped.

He hopped the fence again and drove home, listening to Christmas music the whole way and occasionally sing along to it.

When he got home he went straight to Josh's room, cleaned up the blood and hid the gun in his room. Stephen heard a car door slam shut outside the house and calmly closed Josh's door. He had a worried look on his face as his wife and his two other children enter the house. *"Josh ran away, I've called the police and told the neighbors"* Stephen said this in the saddest way he could. *"Oh No, my baby"*, Mrs. Oliver started to cry viciously. Stephen hugs his wife and tells her that he will be found, though he wished that the cops will never find his body.

Over the next year, Stephen threw out all of Josh's things and boarded up the room, he wanted to remember as little as he could about his son. The thought of what he did kept appearing in his mind. It didn't haunt him though, but instead made him feel accomplished and gave him happiness. This in itself was the reason he murdered his own son, he loved the thrill of the kill and wanted more. Sadly Stephen knew that he couldn't do it again, at least not now, while the police are still looking for Josh. He threw away the stuff because it felt like he was killing again, over and over.

Stephen knew that his desire for blood stood the test of time, and that it could rise up again at any moment, he needed a next victim and soon. He became weary though, every day he saw the raven outside his house and work, enticing him to kill again and soon his opportunity would arise.

Milton Keynes UK
Ingram Content Group UK Ltd.
UKHW010004281023
431464UK00002B/13/J

9 781678 139483